The Secret Society of the Left Hand

Dandi Daley Mackall
Illustrated by Kay Salem

SAINT LOUIS

JF
Mac

*I dedicate this first mystery to my dad,
who passed along to me his love of a good
mystery—and a great God.*

Copyright © 1996 Dandi Daley Mackall
Published by Concordia Publishing House
3558 S. Jefferson Avenue, St. Louis, MO 63118-3968
Manufactured in the United States of America

Library of Congress Cataloging-in-Publication Data

Mackall, Dandi Daley.
      The Secret Society of the Left Hand / Dandi Daley Mackall.
         p.   cm. — (Cinnamon Lake Mysteries ; 1)
      Summary: When Molly and her friends form the Secret Society of the
Left Hand, each member agrees to do a secret act of kindness, but when
someone threatens to reveal the secrets, Molly must find the traitor before
suspicion tears the group apart.
      ISBN 0-570-04792-7
      [1. Clubs—Fiction. 2. Kindness—Fiction. 3. Christian life—Fiction.
4. Mystery and detective stories.] I. Title.
      II. Series.
      PZ7.M1905Se   1996
      [Fic]—dc20   96-14503

2 3 4 5 6 7 8 9 10   05 04 03 02 01 00 99 98 97

Cinnamon Lake Mysteries

The Secret Society of the Left Hand
The Case of the Disappearing Dirt
Don't Bug Me, Molly!
The Great Meow Mystery

I'm not sure how we got famous
as the Cinnamon Lake Mystery Club.
I mean, the Cinnamon Lake part
is easy. That's where we live.
The mystery part is more …
mysterious.

Contents

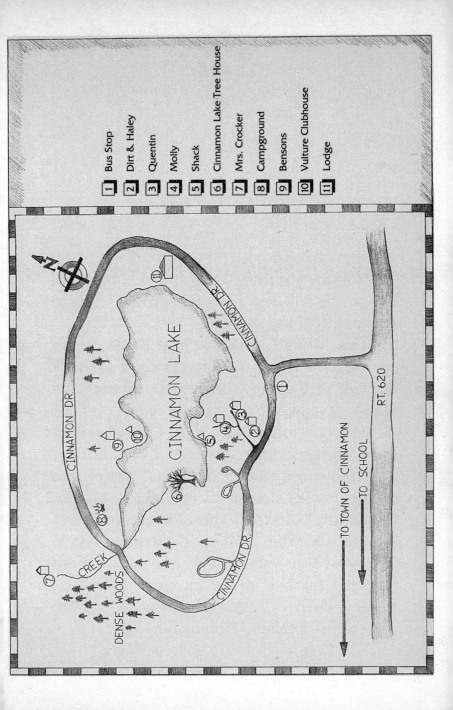

1 Bus Stop
2 Dirt & Haley
3 Quentin
4 Molly
5 Shack
6 Cinnamon Lake Tree House
7 Mrs. Crocker
8 Campground
9 Bensons
10 Vulture Clubhouse
11 Lodge

1

What's Left?

"Run for your life, Quentin!" I screamed. Down the hill I slid. *Zing!* A blast of cold water caught my ponytail.

"Got Molly!" snorted Sam Benson, the meanest kid in our third grade class. "What's wrong? Are you *wilting,* Molly Mack?" he said.

Wilting? I thought. *Oh no! Sam couldn't know about our dried flowers ... or could he?*

Three more shots from Sam's water gun hit me. I never slowed down. I made it to our Cinnamon Lake tree. Then I spun around to look for Quentin. Sam shot one last blast in my eyes! The water stung. Everything went blurry. I blinked my eyes clear. Sam was gone. Then I spotted poor Quentin. "Quentin?" I called. "You okay?"

Quentin was stumbling toward our tree house, wiping his face with his shirt. His belly stuck out. I hoped Sam and his big brother, Ben, weren't around to make fun.

"Outlaws!" Quentin muttered.

I climbed quickly to my branch. There was the handkerchief I'd tied the flowers in. Our club, the Cinnamon Lakers, planned to sell dried flowers for a penny apiece.

"Whew!" I said. "Sam said something about wilting. I was afraid the Vultures found out about our dried flower project."

Sam and Ben Benson and their buddies have a real clubhouse on the other side of the lake. Our group tries to do good stuff. Their club tries to mess us up. They call themselves the Vultures. Good name for them. Vultures feed on other creatures. These Vultures had been eating us alive all summer!

I untied the hankie. "It's okay, Quentin," I said. "The flowers are here." I pulled one out. Nothing but a stem! "What's going—?" I said.

"Molly," Quentin said, climbing to his branch, "please speak in complete sentences."

I pulled out another stem. And another. Nothing but flower crumbs and broken stems.

"All the petals have been pulled off and crumbled!" I yelled.

Quentin grabbed them from me. "Once again we have been foiled." Quentin emptied the hankie. It rained dried flower pieces.

All summer it had been the same. We planned a pizza sale. They found out and had a pizza sale first. We tied logs together for a raft. They untied it overnight. Once we collected four-leaf clovers. Sam Benson pulled one leaf off every clover.

"It will be okay, Quentin," I said. "Summer isn't over yet. This is Tuesday. That leaves us four days. Time enough for one great Cinnamon Lake success!"

Quentin let out a deep sigh. It shook his belly. "It won't work," he said. "The Vultures will find out."

"But how could they?"

Quentin frowned. "Someone is leaking information to the Vultures."

"No way!" I said.

"Think about it, Molly," Quentin replied. "How else could Ben and Sam know every move we make?"

"Quit shoving!" came a whine from below. It had to be Haley.

"Then get out of my way!" barked Dirt.

"It's about time," Quentin yelled down.

Dirt climbed over Haley to her branch. I guess I should say our Cinnamon Lake tree house is more tree than house. We can't get our folks to build a real tree house. So we each take a branch.

"Haley was so scared of Ben," Dirt said. "She made me lead her the long way here. It's her fault."

"Is not," Haley said. She seated herself on her branch. The lowest.

Dirt and Haley are sisters. But they are as different as you can get. Haley always looks smooth. Dirt's more crumpled. Quentin started calling her "Dirt" because she wants to be an archaeologist. That's a scientist who digs up old things for history.

I filled them in on the dried flower disaster. Then we got mad all over again.

"Okay!" I yelled. "The Cinnamon Lake Mystery Club is now called to order!" Don't ask me why they made me president. Quentin is the smart one. He makes the best grades in third grade. Haley is the pretty one. Dirt is only in first grade. But she is the toughest first grader in the world!

Me? I'm average. Average size. Average looks. Average everything. I hate the word *average*.

"Dirt," Quentin said, "we asked you to dress properly for our meetings. That means shoes."

"Put a sock in it, Quentin," Dirt said.

"Come on, guys!" I yelled. "We have less than a week before school starts. The Cinnamon Lakers *have* to pull off something great. And this time, no leaks! Any ideas?"

"I could beat up the bullies," Dirt offered.

"Dirt!" I said. "I mean, any ideas for one last *great* thing for us to do?"

"We could have a Kool-Aid stand," Haley said.

"Kool-Aid stand's a dumb idea," said Dirt. She pushed her hair out of her eyes. "We could sell lemonade."

"Oh, that's brilliant, Dirt," Haley said. All summer Dirt and Haley had done this. Shot down each other's ideas.

"Hold it," Quentin said quietly. He ran his fingers through his wiry hair. He does that when he's working his gray cells. That's what Quentin calls thinking.

"Secret deeds of kindness," he said at last.

Haley, Dirt, and I just looked at each other.

Quentin went on. "The Secret Society of the Left Hand."

"No fair!" Haley whined. "Molly's the only one who is left-handed. That's no secret!"

"No, no." Quentin shook his head. *"Don't let your left hand know what your right hand is doing!"*

I still didn't get it. Quentin looked at us like we were stupid. "It's from the Bible," he said. "It means, when you do something kind, keep it a secret. Don't let anyone know you were the one who did it! It's a way to share Jesus' love without bragging about it."

"I like secrets," said Dirt.

"I love it, Quentin," I said. "The Secret Society of the Left Hand! It's about time the left hand got a break. People get *left* out, *left* back, and just plain *left*. We eat *left* overs. And when we mess up, we're way out in *left* field.

"Have you ever heard of anybody eating *right* overs?" I went on. I couldn't stop myself. "No! We're supposed to eat *right*. There's *right* on! and all *right* and in the *right* and *right* over. It's *right* to be *right*."

"Why should I do *kind* things and keep it

a secret?" Haley whined. "I mean, what's the point? Nobody will even know I did it."

"You'd know. And God would know," Quentin said.

God had always been pretty kind to me— sending Jesus to die for me was *really* kind. "I think it's a great idea!" I said.

"Could we at least tell each other?" Haley asked.

I looked at Quentin. "Yes, that would be appropriate," he said. "But don't you dare tell those Vultures. If *this* secret leaks, one of *us* is a traitor!"

2

Bensons, Bears, and Brownies

If this secret leaks, one of us is a traitor.
Quentin's words hung in the air as if he had performed skywriting from an airplane. The cloud words stayed in our Cinnamon Lake tree house.

Dirt was the first to speak again. "Far out." Haley says Dirt picks up her slang from their dad. He used to be a hippie. After their parents got a divorce, he moved to California.

"The Secret Society of the Left Hand," Dirt said slowly. "Cool! I already know my kind deed."

"You're too little to be in on this," Haley said.

"Am not!" Dirt yelled.

"Are too!" Haley fired back.

"Am not!"

"Are too!"

"Stop it!" I yelled. "Dirt's right." Even as I said *right,* I wished I knew a better word. "We're all in this together," I said. "Each of us has to come up with a kind deed by Saturday. Meet back here to report in every day at four o'clock."

"And don't say a word to anybody," Quentin warned.

We ended the meeting. Quentin and I took the shortcut through the woods. He likes to walk by my house in case my mom will give him something junky to eat. His mom only serves good-for-you food. Rabbit food, Quentin calls it.

I was trying to think up a kind deed. "Quentin?" I said.

"Hmmm?"

"I can't think of a secret kind deed," I said.

"Nonsense, Molly. Use your gray cells. I, personally, am beginning to see a grand plan. My own kind deed." Quentin was staring out at the lake through the trees.

I stared at the lake too. Maybe a great idea would come to *me.*

A couple of little boats glided over the sun-speckled water. I tried to think of some-body old, older than my mom and dad, who might need my help.

All of a sudden, something burst from behind a poplar tree.

"Ha-ah-ah!" he screamed.

It didn't scare me. Not really. But I did jump. I mean, you don't expect somebody to jump out at you from behind a tree. I knew as soon as it happened who it was. Sam Benson! "Very funny, Sam," I said. I tried to act like I wasn't surprised.

"I'll say! You should have seen your face, Molly!" Sam was laughing so hard, he could hardly get the words out.

With his red hair and big green eyes, Sam Benson doesn't look like a bully or a vulture. If he weren't so mean and awful, I suppose you'd have to say he's cute. But he *is* mean and awful. Sam wore green swimming trunks, probably to blend in with the trees.

Poor Quentin must have been more startled than I was. He was bent over, looking for his glasses. He refused to speak to Sam.

"Roar-r-r" came a deep voice from the trees. We don't even have lions at Cinnamon Lake. I looked up just as Ben Benson dropped from the trees. He landed smack in front of Quentin. I think I felt the earth shake.

Ben *does* look like a bully. He reminds me of a bear—not the teddy kind of bear either. He must weigh 400 pounds. Maybe not, but he is the biggest fifth grader *I've* ever seen. When Erin McCarthy moved to our school last year, she thought Ben was the teacher.

Ben brushed his hands on his jeans. He squinted his bushy eyebrows together. "Well, Sammy," he said, "what did we scare up from the bushes here?"

"Why don't you just go scare somebody else!" I said. I was trying to act like Ben didn't scare me. I looked around for Marty, Quentin's cousin. "Where's your pal *Martin?*" I asked. Marty's a Vulture. I'd never call him Martin to his face.

"Why, he's visiting his father, Molly," Ben said. "But he'll be glad to know you missed him."

"You fellows are juvenile and immature," Quentin said. He was wiping his glasses with the front of his shirt.

"Come on, Quentin," I said. I turned my back on the bully brothers. "They're not worth our trouble."

"Why, Quentin!" Mom said when we reached home. "It's so good to see you. Would you like something to eat?"

Quentin's eyes got big.

"Brownies?" Mom asked. We followed her into the kitchen. "Or Oreo cookies?" she offered.

"That would be great, Mrs. Mack," Quentin said. He washed his hands and sat at the kitchen table.

I looked around for my little brother but didn't see him. "Mom, where's Chuckie?" You could tell he wasn't anywhere close. The house was too quiet.

Mom looked tired, like she does when Chuckie's been a wild man all day. He usually is a wild man. "Your brother has *finally* given in. He's taking his nap."

"But it's almost dinnertime," I said. "He'll never go to sleep tonight."

Mom gave me this look like I'd jinxed the night. Then she changed the subject. "So, how did the Cinnamon Lakers meeting go?" She set out little plates. Then she plopped down a bag of cookies and a pan of brownies.

"It was great, Mom. We got this super idea. We're going to start a secret so—OW!"

Quentin elbowed me. As soon as he did, I remembered. Our meeting was supposed to be a secret.

"Start what, honey?" Mom asked. She cut the brownies into one huge piece and one little piece.

"Oh, nothing special," I said.

"I see." Mom set the big brownie in front of Quentin. "How are your parents, Quentin?" she asked, sitting beside him.

"Well, Mrs. Mack, Mother's going through her second preventative childcare phase. She and my aunt have taken my cousin and me off sugar and cartoon violence. She says we fight too much."

"Oh, then maybe I shouldn't be giving you brownies," Mom said. Mom reached for Quentin's plate. He grabbed it with both hands.

"No, really," Quentin said. "Mother thinks it's mostly the Saturday morning cartoons. And anyway, it's okay for me to eat lousy stuff at other people's houses. Mother says we can't educate the whole world."

"No, I suppose not," Mom said. She winked at me.

Quentin finished his junk food and went home. I went to my room, threw myself on my bed, and tried to get my own gray cells working.

3

Be Kind to Killdeer

The next morning, I woke up before anybody—even Chuckie. I wanted to do my kind deed before the next meeting of The Secret Society of the Left Hand. And I had an idea.

Animals. I'd find an animal who needed help. It was the perfect plan! I love animals. And they seem to love me too.

I got dressed as fast as I could, pulling shorts on over my purple swimsuit. Dad was in the kitchen making coffee. I love that coffee smell.

"Molly, what are you doing up so early?" Dad asked.

"Nothing," I said. It wasn't easy to keep my plan a secret. Besides, Dad has lots of ideas. He works for an advertising agency. He has to come up with tons of good ideas every

20

day or they'll fire him.

"Last week of freedom before school starts. I thought you'd sleep in," said Dad.

I shrugged my shoulders. Dad and I sat down to cereal together. I tried to act like I didn't have a big secret. "Dad, tell me about the animals here," I said.

"Like what, Molly?"

"Like what problems do they have?" I was afraid I might have said too much. But Dad didn't look suspicious.

"Same as people," he said. "Biggest problem is getting a date for Saturday night. The married ones fight over the remote control. And the parents—"

"Dad! I'm serious. I mean real animal problems."

Dad wiped his chin with his napkin. "All right. Let's see. Well, we have lots of crayfish."

"Crawdads?"

"Right. They have to worry about the raccoons getting them. But they're pretty fast. And even if a coon catches him, a crawdad can give up one or two of his legs. He's got 10. He'll grow back any the coon bites off."

I started to lose my appetite. "What else, Dad?"

Dad looked at his watch. "Yikes! I've got to fly, Molly." My dad has to drive an hour to get to his office. But he says it's worth it to live at Cinnamon. He grabbed his briefcase and left. He hadn't suspected a thing. He also hadn't been much help.

By the time I got outside, all kinds of birds were chirping. One of them *had* to need my help. I walked to Cinnamon Drive and followed the loop around the lake. I searched the sky and woods.

I'd walked about halfway to our tree house when a bird swooped down at me. *"Killde-e-r!"* it shrieked.

It came at me again. I threw my arms over my head and ducked. A few steps, and two more birds joined the first one. They flew circles around my head. All of them kept screeching, *"Killdeer! Killdeer!"*

That's how I knew they were killdeers. I couldn't think of their real name, but people around here call them killdeers. Once before, killdeers had swooped at me. That time, I ran away as fast as I could. But this time I stood still. Maybe—just maybe—they were trying to tell me something. Maybe those birds needed help—*my* help.

As I crouched, one of the birds flew down a few feet in front of me. Its shrill voice scolded me. Now that I got a good look at the bird, I saw that her body wasn't any bigger than a robin's. But her legs were long, like a sandpiper's. The bird was brown on top and white underneath, with two black bands on her lower neck.

I wanted to see how close I could get. But every time I took a step toward her, she squawked.

"It's okay," I told her. "I just want to help you."

Then I saw it. I almost stepped on it. Right in the road, mixed in with the gravel and stones on the side, was a speckled egg. At first I thought it was a smooth stone. It was gray with black specks, like gravel and tar.

I bent over it to get a closer look. In a circle were three more eggs. No nest, no straw.

All of a sudden, that killdeer mother cried out and almost fell backwards. I was so surprised I couldn't move. She gazed at me with those bird eyes. Then she staggered away. She looked like the wind was blowing her over. But there wasn't any wind. The way she held her wing, it had to be broken.

"Here I come, you poor mommy," I said.

I imagined myself carrying the poor mother bird back home. I'd feed her with an eyedropper. Chuckie could catch worms for her. I'd take care of her eggs. They would hatch and grow. When they were all strong, they wouldn't want to leave. I'd let them stay in my room.

But when I reached the mama bird, she took off. She flew straight into the sky, as if nothing were wrong. She had faked the whole thing! Pretended to be hurt so I'd go after her and leave her babies alone.

I stood there staring into the sky. Then back she came, with her two buddies, shrieking away at me. "Killdeer! Killdeer!"

It sounded too much like "Kill *her!*" I was about to take off, when another whooping yell stopped me. This holler got louder and louder. Ben Benson's racer bike came around the curve. Sam pedaled close behind him. The two of them headed straight for me.

I stuck out my arms like a traffic policeman. "Stop!" I yelled.

Ben kept coming right at me. His handlebars brushed my arm as he raced by. Sam followed him, but not so close.

I looked down. The eggs were inches from my feet. They were okay. I breathed a sigh of relief. But when I looked up, there was Ben Benson. He raced back at me, faster this time. His eyes narrowed. His head stretched over his handlebars. Faster and faster he came.

"Ben, don't!" I screamed. "The eggs!"

I heard the cry of the killdeer above my head. Ben was a blur in front of me. There was nothing I could do.

Crack! Splat! Ben's tires made a horrible, crunching sound. I bolted out of the way. To keep my balance, I leaned backwards. I stumbled. My foot landed on something small, like a pebble. I heard a sickening crack. Without looking, I felt the broken eggshell under my foot. Now all the eggs lay shattered in the gravel.

There was nothing left to do. The killdeers flew silent circles in the sky. I wanted to tell them I was sorry. I hadn't meant to hurt them.

And then I wanted to hurt Ben Benson. I knew I wasn't supposed to feel like that. Jesus says to forgive people who hurt you. How could the Benson bullies be so mean? They *were* vultures, just like their clubhouse said. I was so mad, it felt like burning rocks inside my stomach.

I ran all the way to the tree house. With each step, I imagined I could feel eggshells sticking to my feet. Over and over in my mind I wondered. *Did Sam and Ben know I was trying to do a kind deed? Could they know about The Secret Society of the Left Hand? Was the secret out already?*

4

Dirt's Deed

Quentin was the first one to show up for the Cinnamon Lake meeting. He didn't say a word through my whole story about the killdeer, the hurt mother, the Benson bullies, or the broken eggs.

When I was done and out of breath, I asked, "So, what do you think?"

Quentin sighed. "I think the proper name is *plover,* not *killdeer.*"

"I mean," I began, "you don't think Sam and Ben knew I was trying to do a kind deed, do you?"

"I shouldn't be a bit surprised, Molly. I told you we have a leak. If you want my opinion, I suspect it's Haley's fault."

"It is not!" Haley was here. Her hair was tied up in a pink bow. Her skin was as white as Quentin's was brown. She wore jean shorts.

Haley whined as she climbed to her branch. "If you don't stop talking about me when I'm gone, I'll tell Mother."

"If you're gone," said Quentin, "how will you know?"

"Oh yeah?" Haley always says that when she can't think of a comeback for Quentin. She says it a lot.

"Nobody's talking about anybody," I said.

"Quentin was. He said it's my fault. And it is not." Haley settled onto her branch. "What's not my fault?"

"Centrifugal force and sonic booms," Quentin said. Quentin's going to be a scientist when he grows up.

"Out of the way!" said Dirt. She pulled herself up easily. Dark-haired Dirt was so covered with dirt, you couldn't tell what she was wearing. Her feet were so dirty, you couldn't tell if she had shoes on.

While Quentin made up stories about how Haley set off sonic booms with her whines, I tried to call the meeting to order.

"Listen up!" I said. "Now, we may have

some trouble with our secret kind deeds. This morning I—"

"Not me," Dirt said.

"Not you what, Dirt?" I asked.

"I didn't have any trouble with my kind deed. I already did it."

We all stared at Dirt. She had her legs crossed, boys' style. One foot rested on her other knee. With arms folded, she leaned back on the tree trunk.

"You did your good deed?" Quentin asked.

"Yep."

"No fair!" Haley shouted.

"How do we know you really did this good deed?" asked Quentin.

"Come with me."

We trailed out of the tree house one at a time: Dirt, Quentin, me, and Haley, bringing up the rear. Dirt cut through the woods in back of the tree house. She found a rough trail I'd never seen before. When we came to a deep gully, she stopped.

"Where are you taking us?" I asked.

"We'll get lost," Haley said.

Dirt didn't answer. She reached behind an elm tree and grabbed a big, old vine. It was just like in a Tarzan movie! Before we knew it, she'd jumped off the ground. Clutching the vine, Dirt swung herself easily across the gully.

"Way to go, Dirt!" I yelled. The gully was not that deep. We could have walked down and up it again. But I couldn't wait to try the rope vine. Dirt threw the vine back.

"I'll go next," I said, pushing past Quentin. He didn't fight me for it. I held on to the vine, closed my eyes, and jumped. Over I went! The crackle of leaves stirred under me where the vine dragged the ground. I didn't fly as fast as Dirt, but it felt great. I landed on the other side with a thud, both feet hitting the ground at the same time.

"It's great!" I shouted back to Quentin and Haley. "Come on!"

Quentin crossed next. He didn't look like he was enjoying it.

Poor Quentin didn't quite make it all the way over. Dirt and I had to grab him and pull.

Only Haley stood alone on the other side. "Come on, Haley!" I shouted. "It's fun!"

"She'll never come," Dirt said. Then she turned around and took off walking.

Dirt was right. Haley refused to try the vine. Instead, griping all the way about stickers, she started walking down the gully. I did not want to lose Dirt. So I ran on to catch up with her. As soon as we hit the clearing, I realized where we were. Dirt had taken a shortcut to the campground.

Cinnamon Lake has two big fields that are set apart for campers. People from the city bring their tents or their campers for weekends in the summer. About a dozen families leave their trailers all year round. Those were the only ones still parked there.

Dirt walked to the middle of the campground. She stood, hands on her hips, in front of the trailers. "There!" she said proudly.

I looked around, but I couldn't see anything. Quentin came up and stood with us. "Precisely what is going on?" he asked, panting.

"Well, look!" Dirt said. She motioned with a sweep of her hands toward the campgrounds.

"Dirt," I said, "I don't see anything."

"Yep," she said.

Just then a car drove up and pulled into one of the driveways. A skinny, white-haired man got out. From the trailer came a short, chubby lady. She wore a pink jogging suit and pink hair curlers. She didn't even seem to notice us. Instead, she ran over to the man.

"Harold! Harold!" she said.

"Margaret?"

Quentin and I looked from one of them to the other.

"Harold," she went on, grabbing his arm. "Look!" She pointed around the campground, a lot like Dirt had done for us. Only Harold seemed to understand.

"Land of mercy!" he said. "Why, it's a miracle!"

Quentin gave me a questioning look. I shrugged my shoulders.

"When I came out to get the mail, it was like this. The whole campground! Clean and litter-free!" Margaret sounded out of breath.

"Why, we've been after them for weeks to clean up," said Harold. "What happened? Did they finally send a crew to clean up?"

"No. I called them. They were as surprised as I was. It's like a miracle. As if some angel came down and made our campgrounds beautiful again."

Quentin and I turned to Dirt. I'd never thought of Dirt as any kind of angel. But she had done it all right. Harold and Margaret walked into their camper arm-in-arm.

"Well, why did we come all the way here, I'd like to know!" came a whine behind us. Haley had finally caught up.

"Haley," I said, "Dirt secretly cleaned up the campground. All the garbage and litter are gone. She did it. She pulled off a secret kind deed!"

"Well, that's no fair!" Haley said. "Dirt loves garbage!"

Quentin took the long way back. Dirt disappeared into the woods. So I found myself walking with Haley.

"I'll never think up a secret kind deed, Molly," she said.

"Sure you will," I told her.

"Help me, Molly. You're the president."

I thought about telling her I was having enough trouble of my own. I couldn't even come up with a good idea for myself. But she looked so hopeless. "Okay," I said. "I'll meet you tomorrow, and we'll see what we can come up with."

We came to Haley's turnoff. She started to go, then turned around. "Molly? I know Quentin thinks I'm the leak. But maybe it's Dirt."

I started to protest, but Haley went on. "If the Vultures know about our secret society, how come they didn't bother Dirt?" Then she left.

I wasn't worried about Dirt being a traitor. That kid wouldn't squeal if you stuck needles under her fingernails. But I sure didn't like all the suspicions going around. If we really did have a leak in the Cinnamon Lakers, I decided I'd better find out soon, before suspicions broke us apart.

"You're my best Friend, Jesus," I prayed. "Help me figure this out before I lose all my other friends."

5

The Red Cat Rescue

After supper, Mom made me take my little brother out of the house. She said it was to get him away from television. But she looked like it was to get him away from her.

Chuckie and I kicked rocks down the road. It wasn't dark yet. A few lightning bugs blinked around us.

"Molly!" Chuckie yelled. "Go down there?" He pointed to a ditch filled with stickers.

"No, Chuckie! This way!" I didn't have anywhere to go. So we kicked at a rock and trailed after it. Then I remembered—the speckled eggs.

"Chuckie, don't kick any more eggs—I mean, rocks!" I checked the sky for mad plover.

Behind me came a clacking sound. I knew it would be an Amish buggy. A whole bunch of Amish people live around Cinnamon Lake. They can't have cars or machines, not even TV. I grabbed Chuckie's hand and jerked him out of the road. The clomping of horses' hooves got louder.

"Molly, lookie!" Chuckie shouted.

A one-horse buggy came around the corner. The skinny bay mare was clipping along at a fast trot. Beads of sweat flew off her neck. Three boys in short, black pants, black jackets, and straw hats sat inside the buggy. I recognized the biggest boy, the driver. We'd seen him working in the fields all summer.

"See, Molly!" Chuckie said, pointing at them.

"Chuckie!" I said gruffly. "Don't point!"

When I waved, they all waved back. I stared after them. The setting sun flickered off the metal strip on back of the buggy. I tried to imagine what it would be like to wear black all the time.

Something way down the road caught my attention. A glimmer, something shiny. "Chuckie, did you see that?" I pointed at it.

"Don't point, Molly," he said. He sounded

too much like me to be funny.

We were on a narrow part of Cinnamon Drive. Trees lined the sides of the road. Poplars, maples, and oaks cast dark shadows across the gravel. In between the shadows, something was wrong.

I could see a lump of something. Then shadows covered it and I couldn't see anymore. We got closer. I grew sure it was some kind of animal. I was afraid it was a coon or an opossum. We have so many of them around here. Some are bound to get run over.

I didn't want Chuckie to see. "Chuckie, go pick those wildflowers. We'll bring some for Mommy."

He tottered down the ditch after flowers. I moved in to investigate. What I saw was gold—gold fur. No raccoon has gold fur.

I tiptoed closer. Nothing moved. Finally I could see it clearly. It was a gold, fuzzy cat! I bent over, hands on my knees. The poor thing was covered with something ugly. Ugly and red.

"Oh, you poor baby," I said, fighting the tears. String had wrapped itself around the cat's neck. Strands stretched out in both directions toward the ditches. That pitiful cat must have gotten tangled up in string. Then somebody ran over it and left it to bleed to death.

"What are you doing, Molly?" Chuckie stood beside me with a handful of flowers.

All I could think of was helping the poor, bleeding cat. But it looked like I was too late.

"Stay back, Chuckie," I said. I gave him a little push. I looked around for somebody to help. Nobody was there. It was up to me. I'd have to find the owner. Maybe I'd have to bury the cat myself. Use Chuckie's flowers.

"I have to get him out of the road," I said. I could hardly get the words out. I didn't look at Chuck. I didn't want him to see me cry.

I crouched over the poor cat. And then, I saw his side move. In and out. "Chuckie, he's alive! He's alive!"

The cat jerked. Then he rolled over on his

back. His legs stuck up in the air. Even his tummy was covered with blood. My stomach felt like mush.

I took a deep breath and petted him. My hand stuck to the sticky red globbed over his fur.

Something smelled weird. Chuckie was on his knees beside me now. He reached out to pat the cat. Then he laughed.

I looked at him. How could he laugh at a time like this? His hands were totally red.

"Mmm-m-m-m," Chuckie said. "Ketchup."

That was it! That was what I'd smelled. That cat wasn't covered with blood. It was covered with ketchup!

"Ketchup!" I yelled. I was so loud, the cat leaped up and darted into the woods. Yucky red string trailed behind him.

From the woods came shouts of laughter. I tore through the trees. There were Ben and Sam, sitting on a blanket. The string from the cat led all the way to Sam.

"What do you think you're doing?!" I said, screaming like a killdeer.

"Having a picnic," Ben said. A huge smirk swallowed his round face.

"Yeah," said Sam. "Hot dogs. And ketchup. Want some?"

He held up his hot dog in one hand and a red bottle of ketchup in the other.

"Come on, Molly," Sam said. "Have a hot dog. I see you already have ketchup." Then they laughed even louder. I looked down at my hands and my shirt. I was covered with ketchup.

Chuckie had followed me into the woods. "Mmmm-m-m," he said. "Hot dogs."

All thoughts of secret societies and kind deeds flew out of my head. "Come on, Chuckie," I said. I wheeled around and nearly pulled my brother off his feet. "We're getting out of here!"

"Well, at least you did a kind deed," Ben said.

I stopped in my tracks. "What did you say?" I asked without turning around.

Ben repeated it. "A kind deed. You saved that cat. You did your *kind deed.*"

The way Ben said it left no doubt. I could not believe it! But there it was. The Vultures knew about our kind deeds project. Not only would it be impossible to keep our secret, but I had to admit it. Quentin was right. We did have a leak in the Cinnamon Lakers Club. Somebody was a traitor!

6

Helpful Haley

The next morning, I couldn't quite remember how I got roped into helping Haley. I still had my own good deed to worry about. And now that the Vultures knew what we were up to, it was going to be tough to do anything in secret.

I started out to Haley's. Over and over in my mind ran the question. Who was spilling our secret club business to the Vultures? It didn't make any sense.

Haley met up with me before I reached her house. She looked excited. "Molly! I have an idea. I know what we can do for my good deed."

"What?" I asked.

"Jewelry!" She stared at me as if that one word made everything clear.

"What do you mean, *jewelry?*"

"Lightning bugs! We'll catch them—in jars. Then we'll pull off their yellow lightning parts. We can make bracelets, earrings, necklaces!"

"Haley—" But she wasn't listening.

"Of course, we'll have to keep some of the jewelry for ourselves. That's only fair. Nobody said anything about not doing any kind deed for ourselves. And then—"

I put my hands on her shoulders. "Haley, that's the craziest idea I've ever heard."

"You're just jealous because you didn't think of it yourself," she said. She turned her head to pout.

"Listen to me, Haley. It's wrong to make jewelry out of lightning bugs. It kills them!"

"It does?" she said.

"Yeah. It does."

"Well, now what am I going to do?" she whined. "Thanks a lot, Molly. Some help you turned out to be."

Just then, we heard a loud screech. Sam and Ben Benson on bikes. They slammed on their brakes. Gravel flew! "Well, Sammy," Ben said, "look what we have here."

Sam hopped off his bike. "Why, if it isn't

the kind deed girls!"

Haley slid around behind me. Then she peeked out and said, "I did not squeal to you bullies, no matter what you say!"

"Squeal about what, Haley?" Sam asked.

"About our Secret So—"

"Haley!" I yelled.

"How 'bout you, Molly?" Ben asked. "Have you saved any poor cats lately?"

"Yeah, from ketchup?" Sam asked, cracking up again.

"Why don't you guys just mind your own business?" I said.

"Yeah," Haley echoed. Then she whispered at me, "What do they mean about cats and ketchup?"

"Never mind," I told her.

Ben and Sam looked like they were on their way to their boat. They wore fishing hats with little hooks and feather things sticking out of the brims.

Ben grabbed his neck, like he was choking himself. "Help! Meow! I've been run over!" he screamed.

"Have some ketchup!" Sam hollered back.

My stomach started knotting up all over again. I could see that ketchup-covered cat, those broken plover eggs. How could anyone hurt God's creatures like that!

"It's all Quentin's grandmother's fault for quoting the Bible to him," Haley whispered.

Quentin's granny had a Bible verse for everything. Her favorite was, "A kind word to your enemies is like heaping burning coals on their heads." I couldn't think of anything I'd enjoy more than heaping burning coals on the heads of Sam and Ben Benson!

Then I got an idea. I was all out of coal. And that probably wasn't exactly what God had in mind with that verse. Maybe I'd give Granny a try.

I took a deep breath, forced a smile. "Have a nice bike ride, boys," I said. My voice sounded about a hundred times nicer than I felt. "Haley and I have to be going now."

Sam and Ben stared at us as we walked away. When I turned around to look, they were still standing there. Their mouths were half-open. Ben had his hat off. He was rubbing his head, as if it burned.

Haley giggled. "What just happened here, Molly?"

"Burning coals, Haley," I said softly. "Burning coals."

"Huh?"

I just smiled.

We hadn't walked far when Haley's good mood faded. "Oh, now they'll be watching everything we do!" she whined. "I'll never come up with a kind deed for The Secret Society of the Left Hand."

"Don't give up, Haley. We'll think of something."

"Besides," she whined, "it's just not fair. Dirt's done her kind deed, and I haven't. Hers should not have counted! Just because she cleaned up some old campground and carried junk to the garbage? Dirt loves garbage! You should see her closet! Mother has declared it a disaster area. She yells at Dirt at least a hundred million times a day to clean her stinky closet."

A little bell went off inside my head. "Haley," I said, "I think you just found your kind deed."

7

Closet Phobia

Ten minutes later, Haley and I were standing in a pile of dirty, smelly clothes. It was the worst case of closet catastrophe I had ever seen. A wall of plastic toy pieces covered old shoes and socks. There were balls of every size and shape. Tools. Sticks, rocks, tree bark, and dirt blocked us from going any farther.

I tried to take a step in. Something cracked under my foot. Paper wads or plastic cups.

"Ooooh," Haley moaned. "I never come this far into Dirt's room."

"I can see why," I said, for once feeling sorry for her.

"I'm scared of Dirt's closet," she said.

Why Haley's parents had given Dirt a walk-in closet was beyond me. You sure couldn't walk into it now. "Maybe that's why

Dirt never wears shoes," I said. "How could she find a match in this mess?" This was going to be some deed! "Where's Dirt?"

"I don't know," Haley said in her sour voice.

"When will your mom be back?" I asked.

"Late," she said.

"Good. We're going to need all the time we can get." I plopped down in front of the closet. "Well, let's get to it!"

Haley took some coaxing. Finally, she gave up and joined me. "This is a terrible idea," she said. Carefully she rolled up the sleeves of her white, lacy blouse.

Haley turned out to be better than I was at some chores. I dug deep for all the clothes. Haley threw some in a laundry bag (holding

her nose and looking away as she did it). Other clothes that weren't dirty, she folded. She could fold things great.

Every so often Haley blurted out, "There's my old lunchbox! I looked everywhere for it last year!" or "That Dirt! I thought I lost this jacket at school!"

After about an hour, I announced, "Look, Haley! We can see the floor! We're getting there."

"Why, it's blue," she said, sounding truly amazed. "I never saw the floor of Dirt's closet before. Why does she get a blue closet? Mine is ugly brown. Hey, what's this?" Haley asked.

"What?"

She held up a bulging, red Christmas stocking.

I chuckled. "Look out. She's probably got moldy candy canes in there."

Haley wasn't laughing. She reached in the sock and pulled out a handful of money! Dimes and nickels and pennies spilled out onto the blue carpet. Haley stared from the money to me. "It's full, Molly. Where did Dirt get all this money?"

"Put it back," I said. I wasn't sure why, but

it made me nervous. I started scooping the change back in the sock. Neither of us said anything for a long time. Then we got caught up in cleaning again.

Three hours later, we heard the screen door slam. "Uh-oh," I said. I grabbed the hanging-up clothes and pushed them in. Haley and I scooped up the last of the loose jacks, marbles, and paper scraps from the corners. We were stuffing them into our pockets when the bedroom door slammed open.

It was Dirt. She was holding an armful of sticks.

"Don't you dare put those in the closet!" Haley warned.

"What are you doing in *my* room?" Dirt demanded. She dropped her load on the floor.

"Haley's secret kind deed," I explained.

"What are you talking about?" she asked.

"Come here and take a look," Haley said.

Dirt crossed the room to her closet and stuck her head in. "Huh!" she exclaimed. "Cool. You found my bat." She reached in and grabbed it. Then she started out the door.

"Aren't you going to say anything about the closet?" Haley whined.

Dirt stopped, cocked her head, like she was thinking. "It's blue," she said. And she tore off down the hall.

"Why, that ungrateful—" Haley started after her.

"Wait, Haley!" I called.

Haley turned around.

"It's good that Dirt doesn't appreciate it. This is supposed to be a kind deed that does not get rewarded by other people."

Haley didn't look convinced. I had never in my whole life seen her that dirty. Her hair hung down in oily strands. Grime and fuzz covered her once white shirt.

Outside a car door slammed.

"Your mom's home," I said. "Try not to act funny. She can't know we're the ones who cleaned Dirt's closet."

Mrs. Harrison looked tired, and she looked surprised when she spotted us. "Haley! You look terrible! Change those clothes at once! Now I'll have to wash all over again. You children never stop to think about me."

Something about her voice reminded me a lot of Haley.

"Hello, Molly," Mrs. H. said, as if she'd just noticed me. She glanced around the room.

"Where's Dirt?"

"We're not sure," I answered.

"Maybe she's in her room," Mrs. H. said. She didn't sound too anxious, but she started down the hall. Haley and I trailed along behind her.

Mrs. Harrison stopped when she came to the sticks Dirt had dropped. "Dirt!" she called out. She stepped over the sticks and walked cautiously to the closet. I thought I saw fear in her eyes as she turned the doorknob and opened the closet door.

Mrs. H. let out a loud gasp! It sounded like Haley when she ran across the first spider in Dirt's closet. "It's a miracle," she said in a whisper. Then she called, "Dirt! Roseanna!"

It had never occurred to me that Dirt might have another name. Mrs. Harrison ran past us, out of the bedroom, down the hall.

"What's the matter?" we heard Dirt ask from the kitchen.

"Nothing, my pet," said Mrs. Harrison, almost in tears. "You're an angel. That's all."

When Haley and I reached the kitchen, Dirt was trying to squirm away from her mother's loving embrace. "I'm so proud of you," she said. "Your closet is wonderful!"

Dirt looked up at us and shrugged her shoulders. You could tell she wanted to get out of all the hugging. But she couldn't give us away. "Aw, Ma," she mumbled. "It was nothing."

Haley stormed out of the kitchen. I followed her.

"Well," I said, "we did it, Haley. You should be glad."

Haley looked anything but glad. "Thanks to you, Molly, Dirt is Mother's little pet now. It's not fair."

I didn't know what to say. I stuck my hands in my pockets. Closet junk! I pulled out the marbles and scraps and handed them to Haley. "Here. Might as well finish the job."

Haley made a face, but she stuck out her hand. As I passed her the stuff, a piece of paper floated to the ground. When I picked it up, I saw it had numbers on it.

Haley saw it too. She let everything else drop and snatched the piece of paper from me. "It's a phone number!" she said. "Face it, Molly. Dirt is up to something. First the money in the stocking. Now this! I'll bet she's making money by selling our secrets to the Vultures!"

8

A Tisket, a Tasket: What's in That Basket?

Dirt's money was her own business. But I didn't like Haley's suspicions. She really thought Dirt was selling secrets to the Vultures.

"Haley, don't forget. Kind deeds. Remember? You call it kind to suspect your own sister of treason?" There was one way to put Haley's suspicions to rest. We could look up the phone number. When Haley saw it was just one of Dirt's friends, she'd quit being so silly.

Haley got her mom's directory. We knew it was a Cinnamon Lake number because the first three numbers were the same as ours. So we divided the directory. There weren't that many names.

"I was right!" Haley screamed. "It *is* the Benson number. Dirt's the traitor!"

"Calm down, Haley," I said. I looked. The numbers did match. "There could be a lot of reasons why Dirt has this number. Let's talk to her. Just ask her—"

"No way!" Haley interrupted. "She'll come up with some explanation. And you'll believe her. You're always on her side!"

"There are no sides, Haley," I said. "We're all on the same team." But it was wishful thinking. The Cinnamon Lakers Club was feeling less and less like a team.

Haley wasn't listening. She was looking past me. Out the window.

"That proves it!" she screamed.

I followed Haley's gaze. Outside, it was getting dark. But I could make out Dirt walking down the drive. "So Dirt's leaving," I said. "So what?"

"Do you see that little basket she's carrying?" Haley demanded. "It's the purse Aunt Mary Lou gave her for Christmas. Dirt hates that purse! She said it looks like a basket. Mother and I thought she'd thrown it away. But there she is, sneaking off with it. I'll bet she's heading for the Bensons right now to tell them about my kind deed so it won't count! I'm following her."

I figured I'd better go along to keep the peace. We crouched behind Mrs. H.'s van until Dirt turned the corner.

"See!" Haley whispered. "She's headed for the Bensons."

"Haley," I said, "a lot of people live in that direction. She could be going anywhere."

We followed Dirt, turn after turn, keeping a block behind her. Each turn led us closer to the Bensons. At last we came to their street.

"So who's jumping to conclusions now?" Haley asked.

This time I didn't have an answer. We weaved through trees, over old truck tires and metal scrap. The lawn looked like nobody had bothered to mow it for a thousand years. Five or six beat-up cars littered the lawn.

Dirt stopped on the front step. Haley and I ducked behind a rusty Volkswagen. It was like a car shell. Nothing inside. No wheels.

Dirt glanced over her shoulder. Then she knocked. Three longs. Two shorts.

Lightning bugs flashed around us. Frogs croaked in the distance. Crickets were loudest of all. An owl hooted, and Haley fell back on her seat.

Dirt looked around. Just then the screen door slammed. We couldn't see onto the porch because it was too dark. Somebody said something to Dirt. But we couldn't hear.

Dirt answered, "Yeah, man. Course I got 'em. I said I would."

Dirt set the basket on the step and climbed to the porch. The rising moon shone on the basket.

"What do you think is in that basket?" I whispered to Haley.

"Money, of course," Haley said. "If the Vultures paid that stockingful of cash for our other secrets, Dirt should get a bundle off this one."

"Come on, Haley," I said. "We don't know what Dirt's doing."

"Wake up, Molly!" Haley said. "What's it going to take to make you see it? I'll prove Dirt's the traitor. Then maybe everybody will stop blaming me!" Haley stood up and headed toward the Benson house.

"Haley," I called after her. "Come back."

But Haley kept going. She picked up the basket, flipped up the top, and reached inside.

The next sound was the most bloodcurdling scream I'd ever heard! "Ah-h-h-h-h!" Haley yelled. She dropped the basket but kept screaming.

"Haley!" I ran to her.

The screen door opened and out came Dirt. "What are you doing here?" she said.

The basket lay open on the ground. "My worms!" Dirt shouted. She tried to scoop up the basket, but it was too late. Slimy worms crawled everywhere. Haley had stuck her hand into a pile of earthworms!

Dirt got on her knees and tried to catch them. "Look what you did!" she scolded.

I got down to help Dirt. The screen door opened again. I looked up at the biggest, hairiest legs I'd ever seen.

"What's going on?" said a gruff voice. It was Mr. Benson. He looked like he just woke up. "Where's my bait, Dirt?"

Dirt just groaned. The worms had scurried to the safety of the tall grass.

"You're selling worms for bait!" I said. It was all coming clear. The change, the basket.

"Hey, kid," said Mr. Benson. "No worms, no money." And he went back inside.

Dirt stood up and kicked her basket purse across the lawn. "Thanks a lot!" she said.

Haley still looked like she was in shock.

All I could say was, "I'm sorry, Dirt. Really sorry."

We started walking home. Nobody said

anything. It was like we were each alone, even though we weren't. Then Dirt said, "You thought I was Quentin's traitor, didn't you?"

"I never did," I told her truthfully.

"*You* did!" she said, elbowing her sister.

Haley came to life to defend herself. "It's your fault. Everything is a secret with you! First the money in your closet. Then Aunt Mary Lou's purse. Then this nighttime visit. Quentin was so sure one of us was a traitor. What was I supposed to think?"

"I'd let 'em hang me by my toes before I'd tell them anything," Dirt said. We'd made it to Cinnamon Drive and still hadn't seen another soul outside.

"But Sam and Ben do know about our kind deed project," I said. "So somebody is telling them our secrets."

"Not me," Dirt said.

"Not me," Haley said.

"Me either," I said.

We were quiet for a few seconds. The cricket chirps got louder than ever. Dirt turned to leave. Then she stopped cold. She and Haley looked at each other. At the same time, they said, "Quentin!"

9

Water Voices

When I woke up Friday morning, I said a quick prayer. *God, help me keep the Cinnamon Lakers together.* I knew Quentin couldn't be the traitor. I also knew he had his kind deed all planned. But he wouldn't tell me what it was. It made me mad, as if he thought I might be the traitor. I had to get to the bottom of the mystery. How were the Bensons getting all our club information?

I stepped outside. A loud honking greeted me. It wasn't from a car. Geese! They were back! You could set your calendar to these Canadian geese. It was like welcoming back old neighbors. Some of the geese would stay with us almost all winter. Others kept going.

In the fall and winter I walk down our lane to the bus stop. While I wait, I listen to the geese. I love the way they sound. Like a big birthday party. Only now it reminded me that school started on Monday.

I tore as fast as I could down to our tree house. I could see the geese from there. A dozen geese were checking out the lake. But they sounded like hundreds. I leaned against our tree and waited for more.

Instead of geese, I heard someone say, "Did you see her face?"

I thought I recognized the voice. But I couldn't see anybody.

"No kidding!" Then laughter seemed to bounce off the lake.

Am I going crazy? Hearing voices? I wondered. But I knew those voices ... Sam and Ben Benson!

I jumped up and looked around. Nobody in the trees. Nobody in our tree house. I couldn't see anybody. Yet they sounded like they were all around me.

"Yeah," came Sam's voice. "I thought Molly was going to bust a gut!"

Where were they? I wanted to give them a piece of my mind. My eyes scanned Cinnamon Lake. Back and forth. Then I saw it. Way on the other side of the lake sat a silver rowboat. I could just make out two figures. It had to be Sam and Ben. But how—?

That was it! I could hear them all the way across the lake. Of course! You can always hear better on the water! The geese sound louder when they're in the lake. When we built our raft, we were always hearing people who live right on the shore.

"What kind deeds do you think Molly and Quentin will try today?" Ben's voice sounded like he was shouting the question to *me.*

"Whatever it is," Sam answered, "we'll be there!"

Of course! If I could hear them that clearly, they could hear us. Everything we said on our side of the lake. Everything that went on in our tree house! All they had to do to spy was sit out in their boat.

It was all I could do not to scream at them. But I bit my lip. This was one secret The Secret Society of the Left Hand was going to keep!

I raced back to my house, where I was supposed to meet up with Quentin. I couldn't wait to tell him what I'd found out.

Quentin was eating donuts in the kitchen. Mom was refilling his glass of milk. "Hi, honey," Mom called. "Want a glass of milk?"

"No thanks, Mom." What I really wanted was to get Quentin alone. "Quentin and I have to be going." I tried to catch his attention.

"Relax, Molly." Quentin took another bite of a chocolate donut. "As I was saying, Mrs. Mack, on Saturday my grandmother fed us fried chicken. And she let my cousin and me watch two hours of cartoon violence."

"Oh, and did it hurt you?" Mom asked. She winked at me as she put away the milk jug.

"Kind of," Quentin said. "I mean, the violence didn't get to *me*. But it did my cousin. He beat me up on the way home. Mother says she doesn't know what the world's coming to when you can't trust your own mother."

"Quentin!" I said. "Come on! I need to talk to you outside—on business."

It took two more donuts before I could pry him out of the kitchen.

"Actually, Molly, my friend," he said, "it's good that you stopped by."

"Stopped by? Quentin, this is my house."

"There's a little matter that needs your attention. I—"

"No, Quentin! Me first! I've got something important to tell you."

"All right then." Quentin bowed and waved to me to go on. "What is it? Have you done your kind deed?"

"No, but—"

"Well, then. In that case, I've a favor—"

"Quentin!" I screamed. "Just listen for a minute! I know how the Vultures have been getting our secrets."

He pushed his glasses up on his broad nose. "You know what?"

Then, as quickly as I could, I explained. I told him about the honking and the boat. Sam's and Ben's voices over the water.

Quentin slapped his forehead. "Of course! It's so simple! That's why I must have missed it. Simple physics!"

"What?"

"Physics! Don't you see, Molly? The nature of sound waves. Plus fluids!"

"Sound travels great across the lake?" I said.

"Indeed." Quentin scratched his chin. "Molly, my girl. I need your services this very day. You must perform a small decoy deed for me."

"A what?"

Quentin shook his head. "Pay attention. I must complete my master plan of a kind deed. But I need you to throw the Vultures off the track. Make the Bensons worry about you. Then they will leave me alone."

How could I keep Sam and Ben away from Quentin long enough for him to do his kind deed? Slowly, I felt an idea come together in my little gray cells.

"Quentin, I think I've got it."

A half hour later, Quentin and I met at the tree house. We stood close to the water.

"Molly, I believe I have our last kind deed," Quentin said.

"What is it?" I asked loudly.

"Well, sometimes one has to do things that may not look kind. But in the end, those things become a kind deed. Tough kindness. Do you understand?"

"What are you saying, Quentin?" I was afraid he was sounding too much like a scientist.

"For example," he went on slowly, "take those bully brothers, Sam and Ben Benson. They are unkind."

"Uh-huh," I agreed.

"As mean as they are, they might learn kindness. If someone taught those boys a lesson, why, that would be a kind deed."

"Yeah, but how could we be sure it would be a secret?" I asked.

"I don't see anyone around here, Molly. Do you? Whatever we say will be our secret."

"True." Out of the corner of my eye, I checked to make sure the rowboat was still there. I saw it, and two figures in it were holding still.

"All right then. Here's the plan. You go home and get as many rolls of toilet paper as you can."

"Toilet paper?" I interrupted.

"Yes. Toilet paper. It's called TP-ing."

"Wow!"

"We cover their stuff with toilet paper. String it over their trees. Their boat. Their bikes. Even their Vulture clubhouse. Then maybe they'll get the idea. They shall learn that it's not so funny to play dirty tricks on people."

"Quentin, you're a genius! When should we do it?" I shouted.

"This afternoon," Quentin shouted back. "Meet me down by Bensons' boat dock.

Between two and three o'clock. I'll tell the others. We cannot fail."

"It's a deal, Quentin!" I said.

10

The Decoy Deed

One o'clock that afternoon, I met Quentin at his house. I had to admit it. Quentin had outdone himself this time. He sure didn't need me. He had charts for every stop sign at Cinnamon Lake. He divided them according to sunlight received: (A) full sun; (B) morning sun; (C) afternoon sun; and (D) full shade.

Quentin's grandmother works in a plant shop. Somehow, he had gotten her to give him two boxes full of plants. Quentin knew all of their names and which plant needed what sunlight. All that was left was to stick the flowers in the ground around the stop signs.

"Do you think Sam and Ben fell for the trap?" Quentin asked. He pulled his wagon out of his garage.

"I hope so," I said. "I'll bet they're hiding

away, guarding the Vulture clubhouse right now. Sam would never let his boat get TP'd. They won't bother you. You should have until three o'clock to plant your flowers."

I hung around to help Quentin. Quentin pulled his wagon to a stop sign. He checked his charts. Then he had me pour water before he planted.

Finally, as Quentin pulled up at the eighth and last stop sign, he said, "Molly, it's nearly three o'clock. I need a little more time. You'd better go head them off."

I sneaked through the woods to Bensons' boat dock. My plan was to keep an eye on them until Quentin was in the clear. Sam and Ben's boat was tied up. They never left it tied in the water long. I knew they had to be close by. I looked all around for them but couldn't see anybody. I hoped they hadn't left to find Quentin.

I tried to get the old gray cells working. Maybe Sam and Ben had sat in the boat to wait for us to come TP. They would have gotten tired, sleepy even. Maybe they got so sleepy, they fell asleep.

I tiptoed closer to the boat. If I could just get close enough to peek inside … Just then

I felt a hand grab my elbow from behind. Another hand grabbed my other arm. They lifted me off the ground!

I screamed. "What do you think you're doing?!"

My feet touched ground again. I turned my head and found myself nose-to-nose with Ben Benson. Sam still had hold of my other arm.

"Let me go!" I yelled.

"It will take more than an *average* girl to fool me, Molly Mack," Sam said. "Where is it?"

"Where's what?" I asked.

"You know," Sam said.

Ben held my arm tighter and started to shake me.

"No," Sam told him. "Just ask her."

"Where's that toilet paper?" Ben growled.

"Why, Ben Benson," I said, "since when do you depend on me for your toilet paper?"

"It's not funny, Molly," he growled. "We know all about it."

"All about what?" I asked.

Sam jumped in. "We know what you planned to do! You were going to TP our boat, our trees, and even our clubhouse!

Some kind deed! Well, you won't get away with it."

"Do I look like I'm about to TP anything?" I asked, holding my open palms up in front of him.

Ben peered behind me.

Sam raised his eyebrows and narrowed his eyes. "All right, Molly Mack. Come clean. What have you been up to?"

"We *know* what you were planning," Ben screamed. "We heard you! We were sitting right in our boat. We heard Quentin tell you to meet him—"

"Right!" I said. "You heard us because you spied on us! Just like you did all summer long. You ruined everything we planned!"

"You knew?" Sam said after a minute of silence.

"Well, I know now," I answered.

I wasn't sure, but I thought Sam looked a little sorry.

"So what?" Ben said. "You still haven't told us where the toilet paper is."

I looked at Sam. He almost laughed. "There's no toilet paper, Ben," he said to his brother.

"What do you mean?" Ben asked.

"Don't you get it yet?" said Sam. "We were tricked. Quentin and Molly faked that little talk at the lake. They wanted us to overhear. I'll bet they've been doing their kind deeds while we were hiding here."

"No fair!" Ben said. "You tricked us!"

That time, Sam did laugh. So did I.

I figured Quentin would be done planting by now. So I turned to go.

"Hey," called Sam. "Wait up, Molly." He caught up with me.

"What's the big deal about this kind deed stuff anyway?"

"Well," I said, starting to walk again. "You'll be happy to know that I didn't get to do mine."

"Who cares anyway?" Sam asked. "Will you tell everybody now? Will they give you a reward or something?"

I stopped and faced him. "That's not it. Nobody rewards us. The whole point's to keep our kind deeds secret."

"But I don't get it! Why secret? It doesn't make any sense. Why go to all that trouble if nobody even knows you did it? Ben's been telling everybody *he* cleaned up the campground. Those old people out there think he's wonderful. They baked him cookies!"

"I don't know how to explain it, Sam," I said. "I mean, it started out like a game almost. But it turned out better. You get a good feeling when you do something kind. And it lasts longer or better somehow if you keep it inside. If you don't wait for everybody else to tell you how great it was."

Sam gave me a funny look. I tried again. "Well, you know Jesus says when you help other people, you're really helping Him. It's like having a secret between you and Jesus."

As soon as I'd said it, I wished I could take it back. Now Sam would tease me about God, just like he teased me about being average.

"I've got to go home now, Sam," I said. I turned and ran into the woods.

11

A Powerful Left

Saturday morning. The last meeting of the summer for the Cinnamon Lakers was only minutes away. It would be the last meeting ever of The Secret Society of the Left Hand. I hadn't slept much. I kept thinking about what I'd told Sam. Sam needed to hear about Jesus. So I guess, even if he teased me for the rest of my life, I was glad I said it.

Dad and Chuckie were glued to Saturday morning cartoons. Dad was howling at Bugs Bunny. Mom was putting red marks all over a stack of papers. She teaches summer school at County College. I gulped down breakfast and headed for the tree house.

Before I got to the end of my street, I saw Sam. He was leaning against a big maple tree. When he saw me, he stood up straight.

"Hi, Molly."

I looked around in the trees, in the bushes. "Where's your brother?" I asked.

"Ben? Oh, he's stuck in front of the TV. He watches cartoons until his eyes bug out."

"So does my brother," I said. "But at least he's only three." I didn't mention that Dad was keeping Chuckie company.

I kept walking. To my surprise, Sam kept walking beside me. I glanced to make sure he wasn't about to trip me. No hidden ketchup bottles.

Neither of us said anything for awhile. Finally Sam said, "Molly, you know what you said yesterday?"

"What?"

"About kind deeds and Jesus an' all?"

"Yeah?" I said. I prepared to be teased.

"It made sense," Sam said.

"It did?" I checked Sam's face. He wasn't laughing.

"Yeah," he said. "It did."

"Great," I said. "Jesus makes a lot of sense, Sam." I took a deep breath and asked Jesus to help me keep going. "Jesus loves you so much He died for you." Sam didn't say anything. But he smiled.

We were passing our first stop sign. "Look!" I said. "See what Quentin did— Oops, you can't tell anyone, Sam. Nobody's supposed to know who did it."

"Except Quentin. Right? And Jesus?" Sam seemed excited, like he'd just been let in on a huge secret.

"Right," I said. I wondered if Quentin would be mad at me for telling Sam about the flowers.

Sam kicked a rock and ran ahead after it. "They're here!" he yelled.

He pointed to three bikes leaning against a tree. That's where Haley, Dirt, and Quentin always park.

"I gotta go now, Sam," I said. I started down the hill.

"Molly?"

"Yeah?" I called over my shoulder at him.

"Oh, nothing." I heard leaves rustle as Sam started to leave.

Quentin and Haley would kill me. But they would probably kill me anyway for not doing my kind deed. "Wait, Sam!" I yelled. "You want to come?"

"Really?"

"Sure," I said. "Why not? It will probably

be my last meeting as president anyway."
Maybe it wouldn't be so bad to have Sam
along. I wouldn't be the only one there who
hadn't done a kind deed.

When we got close, I decided I better
warn everyone. "Here we come!" I shouted.
"Quentin?" No answer. "Haley? Dirt?"

Still no answer.

"I know they're up there," I told Sam.

Just as we got to the tree house, a shout
came from above. "Hurray!" Then Sam and I
were pelted by little green apples.

"Hey!" yelled Sam. "What's going on?"

The Cinnamon Lakers dropped out of the
tree house in front of us. Quentin's face melt-
ed into a frown. "What's *he* doing here?"

"Yeah!" said Haley.

Dirt put her fists up.

"It's okay," I said. "Sam just wanted to
hear about your kind deeds."

"He what?" Quentin asked.

"Trust me," I said. "Anyway, what are you
guys throwing apples for?"

"Party," Dirt said.

"We didn't have confetti," Quentin said.
"So Dirt talked us into using apples."

"We even have treats," Haley said. "Too

bad Quentin's mother is the one who sent them."

"Pickled pears," said Quentin.

I looked at Sam. He shrugged his shoulders.

"For The Secret Soc—" Quentin stopped himself. He glared at Sam.

"It's okay," I said. "Sam knows about it."

We climbed our tree house. Quentin handed up yellow, pickled pears.

"To the Cinnamon Lakers!" Quentin said. He raised his pear in a toast.

"To never letting your right hand know what your left hand is doing," said Haley.

"Right on," said Dirt.

"For successfully ending The Secret Society of the Left Hand," Quentin said.

"Well, almost successfully," I added. "Maybe I better go home and let the rest of you party." I started to do just that.

"What are you talking about?" asked Quentin.

"Kind deeds," I said. "Dirt cleaned the campground. Haley cleaned Dirt's closet. You planted beautiful flowers all over Cinnamon Lake. But I didn't do anything."

"But you *did!*" said Quentin. "More than any of us, to tell the truth."

"I did not. Well, there was that ketchup-covered cat, but—"

"Not that!" Quentin said. "For one thing, you kept us from blaming each other."

"I don't get it," I said.

"Look, Molly," Quentin explained in his scientist voice, "I couldn't have done my kind deed without you. Why, if you hadn't kept those Benson bullies—" He stopped and looked over at Sam.

"It's okay. You're right," Sam said.

Quentin kept one eye on Sam but continued. "You made it possible for me to plant flowers."

"I must admit, you were helpful to me in that closet kind deed," said Haley.

Dirt banged on Haley's branch with a long stick. "They weren't even going to let me be part of the Secret Society. You made them!"

I couldn't think of anything to say.

"And look at me!" Sam said. "I'm here! And I'm not even doing an unkind deed!"

We all laughed. For once, I felt much better than *average*.

"Wow," I said at last. "Not only didn't my right hand know what my left hand was doing. Not even my left hand knew!"